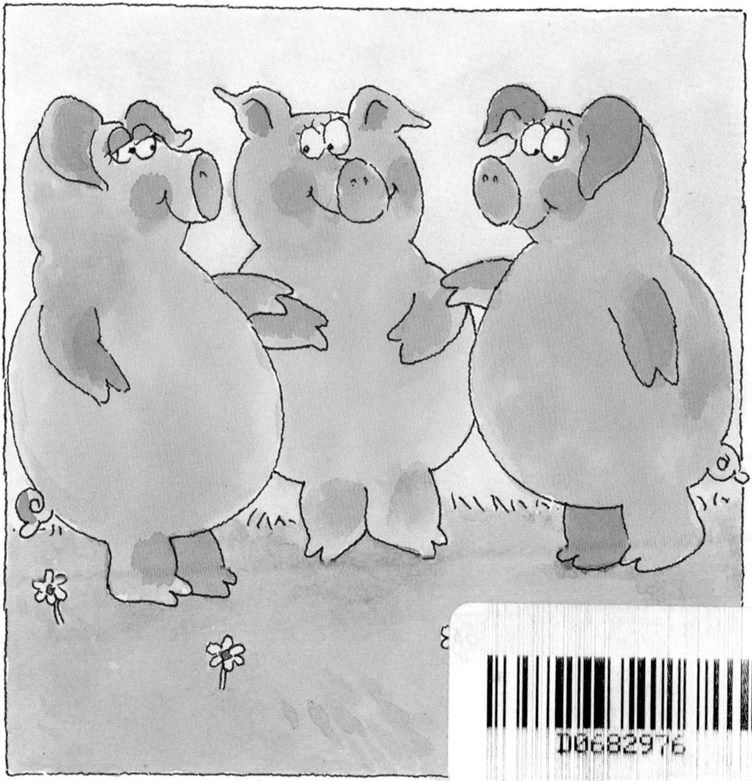

Three pigs

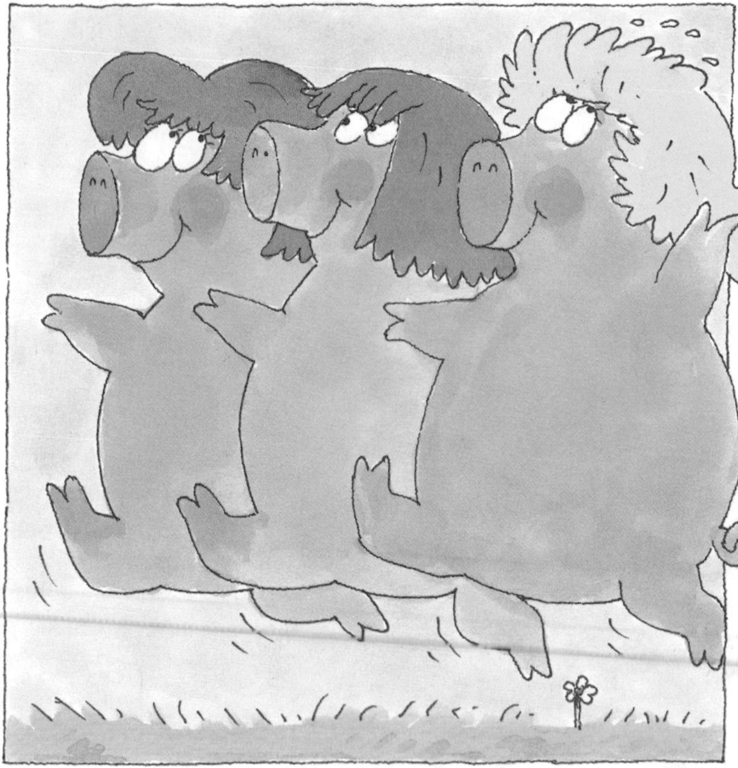

have three wigs.

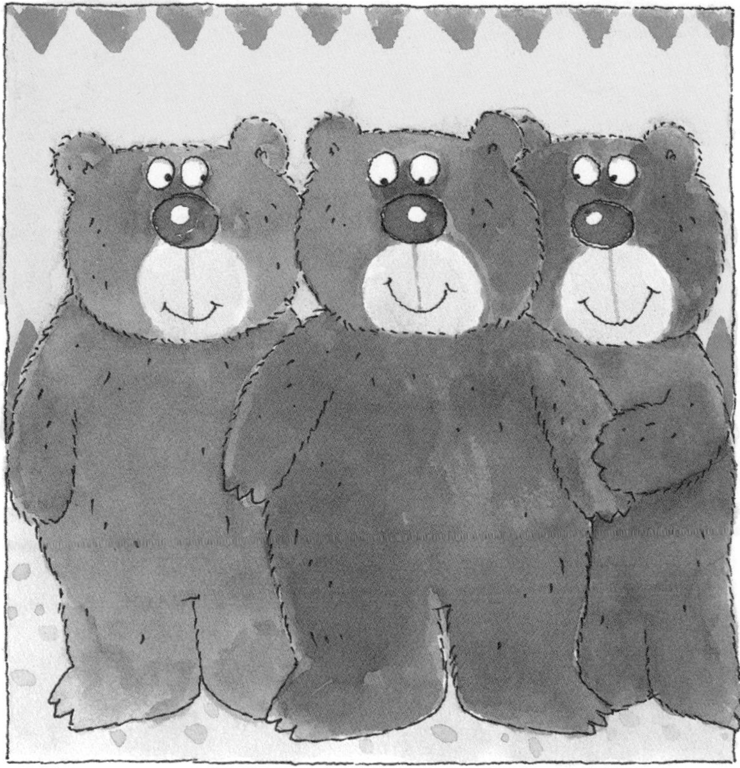

Three bears

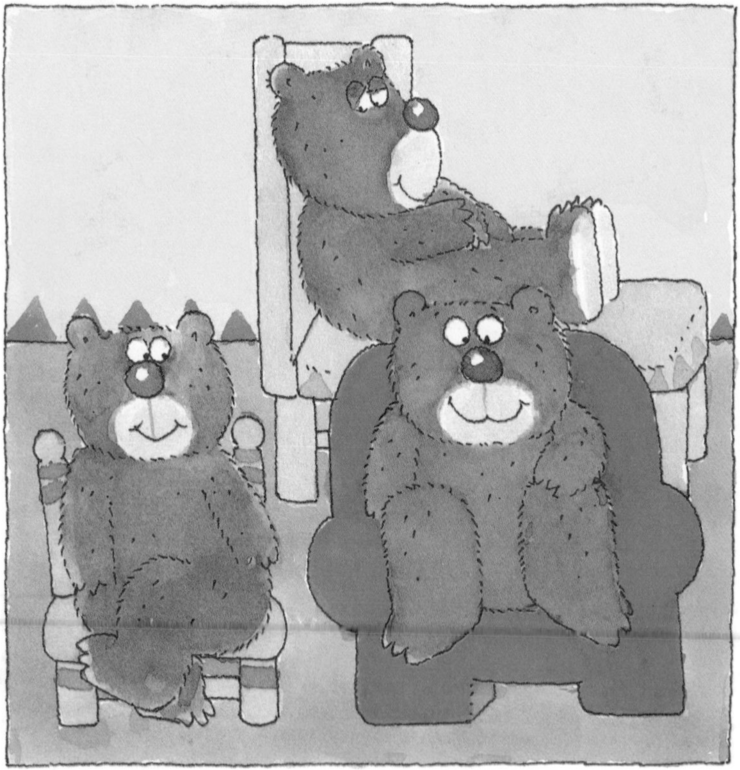

have three chairs.

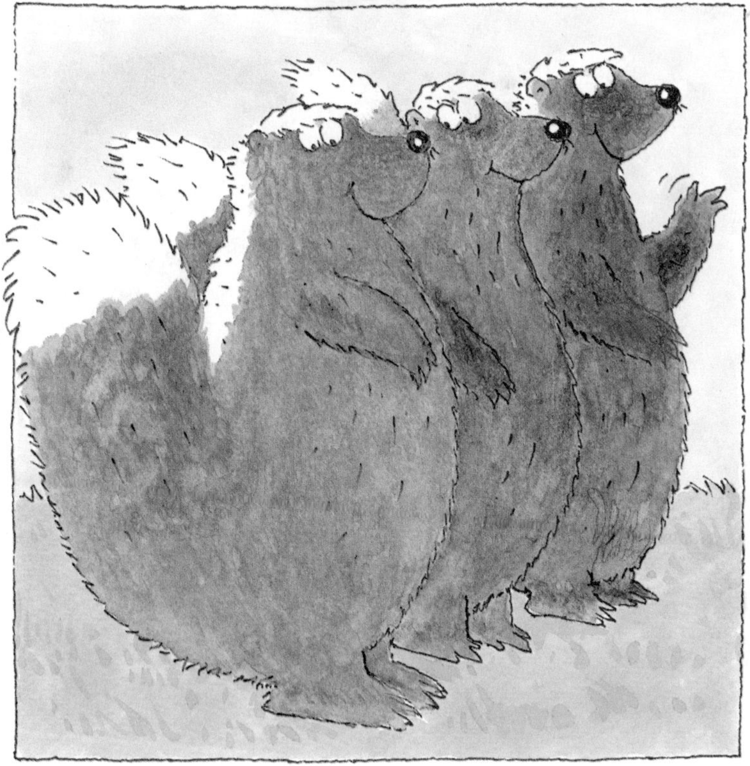

Three skunks

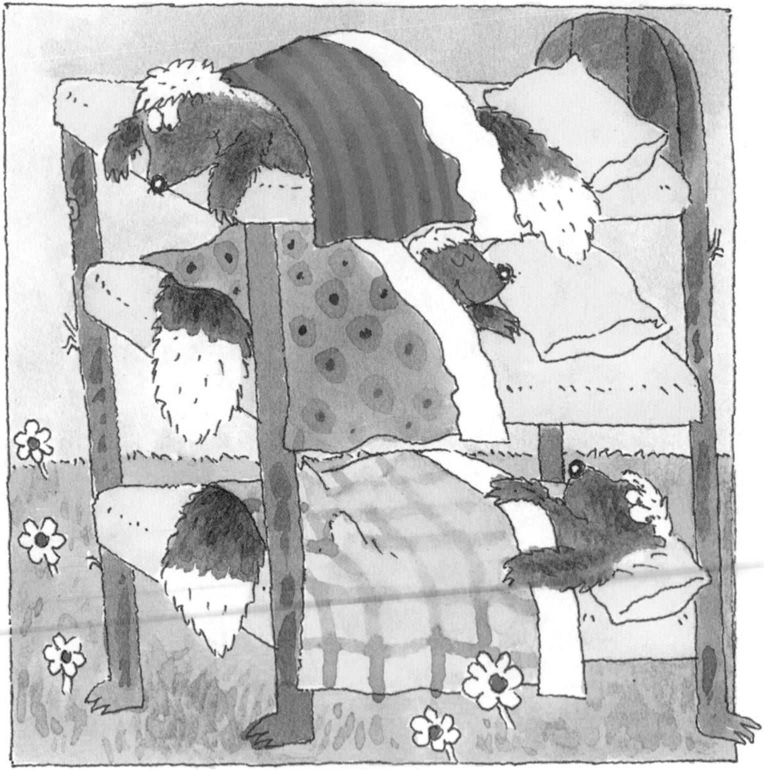

have three bunks.

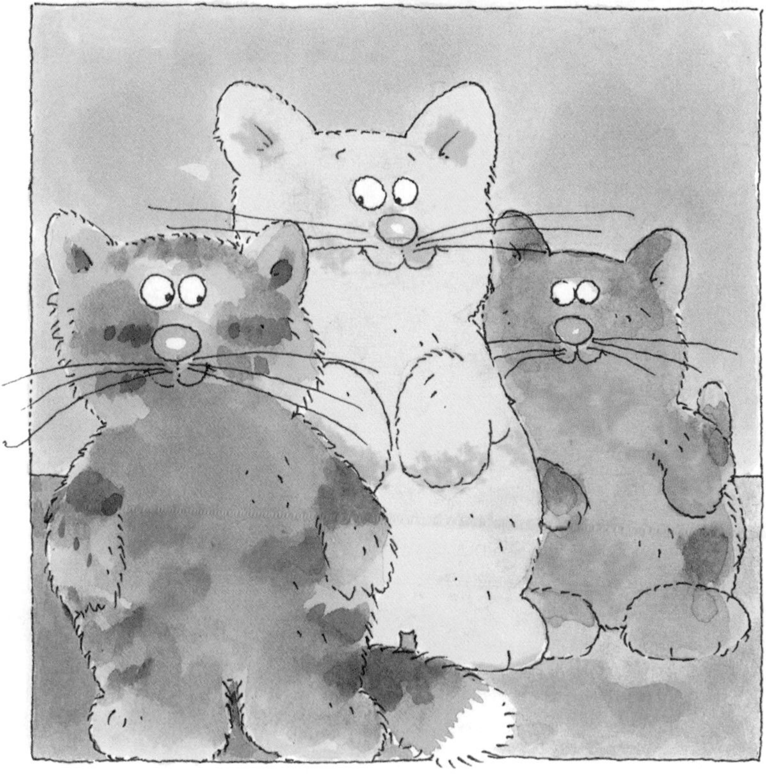

But three kittens

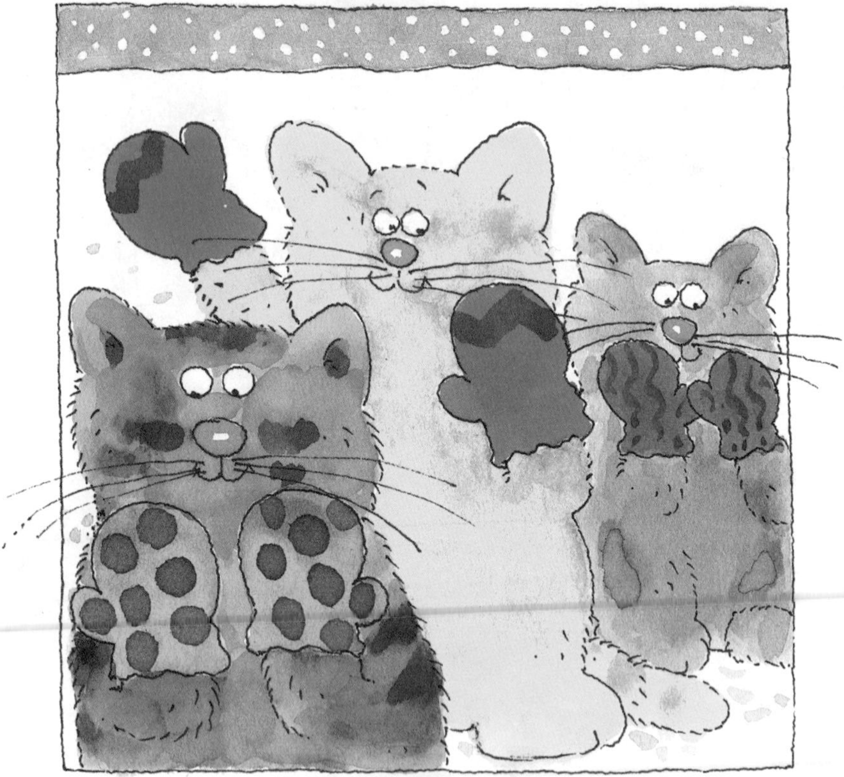

have 6 mittens!